Looking Both Ways

A Breakthrough Book

No. 45

Looking Both Ways

Poems by Jane O. Wayne

University of Missouri Press
Columbia, 1984

University of Missouri Press, Columbia, Missouri 65211
Printed and bound in the United States of America

Library of Congress Cataloging in Publication Data

Wayne, Jane O.
Looking both ways.

I. Title.
PS3573.A94L6 1984 811′.54 84–2201
ISBN 0–8262–0454–6

Production of this book was funded in part by a grant from the National Endowment for the Arts.

Grateful acknowledgment is made to the editors of the following magazines in which these poems first appeared: *American Scholar*, "Slipping"; *Ascent*, "Tooth and Nail"; *Driftwood East Quarterly*, "Postpartum"; *Envy's Sting*, "Street Litter"; *Kansas Quarterly*, "The Only Cure"; *Massachusetts Review*, "Playing from Memory"; *Poetry*, "With Solitude," "Braiding Your Hair," "First Freeze," "Autumnal Equinox," and "The Family Album"; *Poetry Northwest*, "Kitchen Midden" and "Looking Both Ways"; *River Styx*, "Convalescence" and "Blood Feud," which first appeared as "Microbes"; *Road Apple Review*, "Abrasions"; *Windless Orchard*, "A Physical Examination" and "Interval"; *Wisconsin Review*, "Anticipation"; *Webster Review*, "Genesis," "Outpatient," and "Refuge"; *Woodrose*, "Facing Widowhood."

"Premonition," which received Honorable Mention in the Jones Foundation National Poetry Competition 1982, appeared in the anthology of winners. "The Only Cure" and "Playing from Memory" appeared in the 1984 *Anthology of Magazine Verse and Yearbook of American Poetry*.

"The Eavesdropper" and "Lapsing" are forthcoming in *Ploughshares*.

The quotation from Gabriel García Márquez is from *One Hundred Years of Solitude*; that from Miguel de Cervantes is from *Don Quixote*; that from Wallace Stevens is from *Esthétique du Mal*; and that from Huston Smith is from *Religions of Man*.

FOR SAM

The Devins Award for Poetry

Looking Both Ways is the 1985 winner of The Devins Award for Poetry, an annual award originally made possible by the generosity of Dr. and Mrs. Edward A. Devins of Kansas City, Missouri. Dr. Devins was President of the Kansas City Jewish Community Center and a patron of the Center's American Poets Series. Upon the death of Dr. Devins in 1974, his son, Dr. George Devins, acted to continue the Award.

Nomination for the Award is made by the University of Missouri Press from those poetry manuscripts selected by the Press for publication in a given year. David Wagoner was the judge for all poetry selections made in the Press's Breakthrough Series for 1984 and 1985.

Contents

First Freeze

The last chrysanthemums
sit in a jar on the breakfast table.
Green tomatoes line the windowsill.
The back door's closed.

Already the tea is tepid in my cup.
I sip the room's temperature.
Wool, mothballs, their odors chill me.
Inside. Outside. It's everywhere.

Privet, forsythia, hydrangea, mulberry,
old rags wrung out by the night
now hang drying in their branches.
I don't know where to start.

The ornamental pool traps yellow litter
from the birch. Ash and sycamore leaves
tangle with ivy.
And I'm all entropy with a rake.

Across the street, a door slams
and a dog, nose to the ground,
zigzags over the lawn
like a pencil scribbling wildly.

Genesis

We are the lazy carpenters
who bought this apple tree
assembled
and built our garden
in a single afternoon.
We merely hammered
into soft earth
this club-footed nail.

Under the Apple Tree

One bite and I'm through, wasteful
as these squirrels.
My teeth marks roll with theirs in the dirt.

Things drop that I don't touch,
the ripe beside the rotten.
A foot away from me,

an apple hits the ground
and cracks its skull.
Another falls off in my hand like a doorknob.

I crouch disguised in silence, a dreamer
rooted to the spot.
I could be next.

Maybe if I stand perfectly still in the shade
I will be shade.
A sudden move and no one would notice.

I hold back flight like a sneeze.
Even the basket tugs at me
till one foot strays

and sinks in pulpiness.
All around me, flies gather to celebrate.
Sweetness rises from the ground.

Kitchen Midden

After the crash
I feel as empty as the gold-rimmed plate at my feet.
Whom can I blame to break the silence?

I hold the halves,
two continents lifted from a map.
How close they fit along the jagged seam.

I think of glue, eleven plates at the table,
a molar splitting in a recurring dream.
Only the fissure is complete.

This time, the porcelain breaks against the air,
collapses, like a plain along a fault,
but silently.

I test the fragments to the window.
Blurred, the gold design shows through.
So do my fingers.

In such bright light, maybe I'm translucent,
a piece of bone china.
On the path to the alley, a rock outstares me.

Even the trees must know.
When I walk, the twigs snap underfoot.
Two shards rattle in this bag of trash.

Weaknesses

"The greatest poverty is not to live in a physical world."
—Wallace Stevens

Sometimes you leave your cup half filled,
dishes in the sink, on the cutting board
peeled potatoes graying.
You can't finish anything.

Going there the words rush
but coming back you let the oars drag,
let the reeds rubbing under the boat
do away with your small talk.

If it had been otherwise
you could have stayed in an easy chair,
crossed your legs without your foot tingling
or your heart on pins and needles.

No sap in your branches,
nothing for a wind to stir—
you could have pollarded the long afternoons,
kept your hands folded on your living-room-lap.

But at the front door
after standing up too fast
you wouldn't reel—or when your head clears
wouldn't stop longer than is necessary,

your bare feet on the tiles,
the door wide open,
just to hold another morning
like the cold milk-bottles in your hands.

You know your own weaknesses.
Yesterday in the rain taking the shortcut
to town, the old path
through the churchyard where the grass, moss,

and even the names and dates on that slab
fallen like a paving stone
have worn away—something in you swerved
but something else kept you on the path.

At night, like a child sent to bed,
you watch hungrily
the last inch of light under the door.
You can never get enough.

In April

("ecstasy" from Greek *ekstasis*, from *existanai*, to displace, drive out of one's senses)

A man gets on and pushes a button.
When the doors close, my hands do too.

Rising, I am perfectly still,
a dress hanging in a closet.

I turn my eyes off,
but my sense of smell returns.

Is it smoke from his pipe
or the thick air of spring in the elevator?

For a moment I am weightless,
half of me ascending, half abandoned,

till the elevator empties at my floor,
and I lean broomlike in the corner.

Residue

This is the last sip
the lukewarm tea
the leaves littering the tongue.

You make promises
like the man who sprinkles salt
over everything.

Nothing will grow on this table.
Even the slice of bread
curls away from your plate.

It's the white moth in the garden
and overhead a sun
slowly dying in its socket.

Routine

Today was no different—
getting up at seven, brushing my teeth,
my hair, washing my face—
except the towel, that erasing
near my ear, over my cheekbone,
it stopped me in the mirror.

Maybe I was looking
for a crack in habit
but nothing broke.
It's always the same
white tile, green towel,
black specks in the silver.

Even at the dinner table
ribbons all untied,
gifts undone,
I hold the last torn wrapper
wondering what's left
to open in my life.

Sometimes I can't help wanting
something more.
In bed watching the moon
slide between curtains, I can't sleep
like a drawer jammed
neither open nor shut.

Postpartum

I'm a cutlet on a hard table
pounded thin
with my own mallet.

A mean dog has me cornered
growling low
so no one else can hear.

All night my limbs clatter
like cutlery
against an empty plate.

This is my winter
flat on my back
under a cold white blanket.

Maybe it's snow
and I'm the empty mitten
that lost its child.

Interval

This house could ruin us all.
Tonight's cake falls
like a cat flattened on the road.

While you walk the baby
my spoon runs circles
over a low, blue light.

Onions, garlic, basil, thyme—
their odors fail me.
They are short candles in a dark room.

This is the same kitchen chair,
straight-backed and wooden,
the same crossed leg kicking the air.

Outside the window in the sycamore
a cardinal sits
like a brilliant flame that doesn't flicker.

Even the cat stands still.
I hold my breath.
I see the green around the red.

Now I hear the bird,
the slamming of the front door,
the rinsing of my cup.

Solstice

This is the shortest day;
the longest night approaches.
From the shore, I can hear the lake creaking
under skaters, the iced branches
cracking their knuckles overhead.

Some boys stand guard
by a trash-can, waving their hands
over it, letting some sparks
escape, letting a black dog bark
white smoke at them.

Now as the earth reaches
its most northern point, snow piles
on snow—my toes stiffen from it,
my lower lip splits down the middle
like a worn trouser knee.

Walking home, our youngest skater
whines with the wind.
She goes limp in my arms
slipping the way the blanket
does from our bed.

Maybe we only went out
so we could come back again,
striking matches, sipping out of small cups,
watching the early sky steep
from an armchair.

Before School

In the pan where the eggs are shallow
a wave of thickness starts and spreads everywher
The wooden spoon I hold is surrounded.

Silence must come to my kitchen.
The way I turn my face when the bacon splatters
she could turn from me.

She ignores her plate.
Two milk teeth rattle in her hand.
They tumble to the table's edge like dice.

She's at the bottom of her glass,
blowing on a straw,
wanting nothing more than bubbles.

Hugging me, she pulls her arms off quickly
the way I tear off bandages.
The screen door bangs behind her.

On the porch steps, she leaves her name
scrawled in pollen dust, leaves her glass
to sour in the sun.

Hands pocketed, eyes on the ground,
she takes uneven steps
skipping the cracks in the sidewalk.

Braiding Your Hair

Last night I found you walking in your sleep.
Stopping near the stairs,
staring right at me,
you answered someone in your dream
then went to bed.

Now brushing the night out of your hair
I keep catching on knots,
not your words, they're forgotten,
but your face so fugitive, your eyes
at pointblank range a stranger's,

the mystery, not just yours but mine,
the day and night in all of us.
Your hair between my hands,
your back to me,
I separate the strands and braid them.

The Family Album

The spine creaks when you open it;
the thick pages flap
like black wings between your hands.
You don't stop
until you notice one of her,
sitting on a wall, a girl your age
in braids, a school uniform—
white middy-blouse, dark tie,
dark stockings on her dangling legs.

You must be studying the mouth
they say you have,
the grandmother you never knew.
You even rub your hand
slowly over the shiny girl
the way I do a window
when I can't tell which side
the dust is on—
before you let the cover drop.

In an Unmown Meadow, near Newtown

On the way to the next farm
the path we trample in the hay seems straight
till looking back we notice
that it wobbles
like a child's penciled line.

Always short of the truth,
it's what keeps us going.
Our children too.
Running knee-deep through the hay
they gather wildflowers—

whites, yellows, lavenders by the handful,
then at the stile they stop
as if the field in their arms
were not enough. They want names—
stitchwort, buttercup, red clover—on their lips.

Getting By

After the sea, the hot sand
and the long ride home
when they carried us to our dark beds
I used to pretend
that night was only the Venetian blinds
drawn tighter and tighter

that if I wanted to
I could open them like tired eyelids
and the afternoon would go on and on
the way the coastline does.
Maybe I still pretend
about the dark

as if I could get by
without touching it—
the way crossing the cold floor
of this changing room
my feet still cringe
from the puddles and grit.

Turkish Ruins

First the ice cubes leave.
Then the fingerprints wash away.
No proof of our smiles remains on the rims.

Dry air sips dregs from our glasses.
White marble, white sand,
they glare at us.

And these black clouds doing their dirty work,
why do they follow us?
The air is ruined with their buzzing.

None of us is spared.
We drain slowly
like the empty cows hanging in the market.

All night the shutters defy us.
They bang like hammers
nailing down our door.

Hospital Visit

His last meal
washed from his mouth,
the bars criblike on his bed,
his soft breathing

also like a baby's,
motionless
but moving further than the eye
in this penultimate sleep,

his thin skin, papery and wrinkled,
he's an old envelope
with no letter,
nothing for his daughters

unless a note
is caught in a corner,
some word, some syllable
sealed in his throat.

The Eavesdropper

That small girl crouched
on the top steps to listen
is still waiting to hear her name
on their lips, to come alive
like a deck of cards
shuffled in their downstairs hands.

She's still motionless
outside the living room, straining
to catch some hint
that no one drops, still in that hallway
dwelling on their talk
as a thumb does a rough fingernail.

Lapsing

When she stops us on the street
the white hair is what we see first,
the careful set and comb of it,
and then the three keys
strung around her neck on a shoelace,
the winter coat, the bare legs.

She can't say how many streets it's been,
how many cracks in the pavement,
look-alike doors.
Her own house she misplaces
like a pair of gloves, then just as absently
pulls out her name

as if she's had it all along
like that handkerchief in her coat pocket,
her address, too, where a man answers
tired of it—
this old woman losing herself
the way he might a pen or pencil.

She may be off the streets now
but she's still loose in our minds.
There's no forgetting her,
no hanging up on her threat
in the middle of the night,
no putting her off like a bad debt.

Blood Feud

They want to open all the windows
in this house
and let the wind cough on me.

They want to sweep me out
with the cat
to wander alleys in the rain.

They want to cut me down
and dig me out
by the roots.

They call me down to the river.
They want to send me
out to sea.

They want to take me by the hand
to a quiet park
and give me flowers.

They would spit me out
like a watermelon seed
but I would grow in the ground.

Outside

This sycamore when I come close
loses its birds.
The air's confused with flapping.

I'm the misfit in this garden,
like a housecat that climbs a tree
and can't get down.

Green leaf, green caterpillar,
where's my place? The lawn is spongy,
the brick ledge slippery with moss,

and puddles occupy the lawn chairs.
I'd call, but the dog won't come.
He's lapping water from a bowl of mud.

A branch rattles in the sycamore.
A nervous ripple runs along the privet's spine.
So what if the squirrels watch all my moves.

Hard plums, hard peaches,
apples still too small—
I won't need an alibi.

Anticipation

1

The house is cold.
I'm hiding under blankets.
My neck gets stiff.

Like a leaf on a potted plant
maybe I will die
from the top down.

2

Someday if I live alone
with a dozen eggs
and a loaf of bread a week

will they come and find me
with my forefinger stuck
in the handle of a cup?

3

Ivy takes the neighbor's lawn
without a struggle.
Will I sit in silence

when wisteria
scratches at the eyes
of this house?

4

If they come tomorrow
they won't get much.
I'll be stubborn

living in a crack
in the pavement
like a dandelion.

In the Woods

Out here, it all happens so fast:
the frozen pond opening one eye for the dog,
the man with a stick appearing
on the edge of the ice—lying down,
stretching himself out like a lifeline
on the hellish pool, trying with the stick
to fetch that Cerberus
from the underworld

until the barking
then the bobbing in the water stops,
until there's nothing more to see—the dark pupil
in the glassy eye is empty—
nothing more to hear except that stick
dropping on the ice. The woods
around the pond resume the silence
of a book closed on a myth.

After the Fact

The mind's porcelain keeps shattering
at her feet. She can't get away from it.

It's in the cup she holds, in the plate
she carries from the table.

Even in the dark, she stumbles
on the blunt-edged fact like a footstool.

Winter-colored, sticklike
he reappears leaning on a stick

pauses in her mind to catch his breath
before he inches off without her.

She wasn't there, but she can see him,
tripping on nothing. She can hear it

when the bottle topples from her reach,
when a broom falls headfirst from the closet.

Tomorrow she will crack another morning
on the rim of a bowl and stir the memory

until it slips from her at the table
the way the napkin does from her lap.

Facing Widowhood

Someone has drawn a shade
in my neighbor's window.
I listen to the radio for news:

the same drought,
the same slow damage in the distant fields.
Nothing changes my mind.

I pour tea and wait.
Slowly the cloud
passes over the cup.

There is no detour.
I climb carefully
to silence the steps.

The old boards sing
when I least expect
never the same song twice.

With Solitude

"The secret of a good old age is simply an honorable pact with solitude."
—Gabriel García Márquez

If I stare too long
the dregs congeal in the bottom of this cup.
Maybe the brindled cat holds me prisoner.

Sometimes a week can pass.
I don't go outside. I keep my secrets to myself,
let dirt accumulate beneath my nails.

Always the same chair,
until the stuffing sags, the pink upholstery thins.
The damage is a perfect fit, my image in intaglio.

And in my lap, the cat curls.
I feel the warmth through my skirt,
on one side of my face, the heat of the lamp.

Tail arched, the cat leaves the room.
Nothing moves
except the darkness in the hall.

Outnumbered by the minutes,
I hold my own with weak tea.
Sipping. Sipping.

I can outstare the night, the winter too,
outlive these teeth if I have to.
Already bare-boned stems show on the asparagus-fern.

Its thin leaves curl on the carpet,
like old hair, dry and colorless.
Adding water doesn't help.

Nor does the broom.
I don't have to try anymore.
Solitude is two smiles, the mirror's and mine.

At Dusk

Sometimes I stroll at dusk, just to hear
cutlery clinking on china, strangers

stacking dinner dishes, laughter.
This is the season for open windows,

for barefoot girls shrieking over the lawns
after lightning bugs. And in a jar

the greenish-yellow lights
severed from the flies are still flickering.

When I come close, they all glance away.
I must be one of those,

a hag caught humming under her breath
the same song over and over.

A man approaches hauling a leash.
His shapeless dog scrapes along the pavement.

Without slackening, the man turns
slightly toward the curb and spits.

In the street a boy heaves a football.
Another misses it. The distance

is the game between the players, between the head
and hand, between this moment and another.

Abrasions

Through this window
I watched the morning rain
take the blossoms from the peach tree.

Now the roof leaks.
From the pitch licking slowly down
rain comes to eat the bricks.

I cringe under a shawl.
I watch the cat
pacing back and forth over the carpet.

This is my last house,
my last shoe size.
Only the hole in my sock grows larger.

At night when the moths and beetles
scratch against the screen
I move over.

Street Litter

Instead of rocks
some strange river passing over this land
deposits broken glass.

A sheet of newspaper
momentarily clings to a parking meter
till a gust loosens its grip.

Dry branches groan in the wind
and a pack of boys howls
snapping twigs like fingers.

At the bus stop a girl with books
and a man whose candy wrapper flies overhead
ignore each other.

A tinseled tree rolls into the street.
Like a deaf dog, it strays
unhurried by the honking.

The Tomato Man

On Wednesdays if she shops in the open market
she has to pass that stall
where a man scowls, waiting for a buyer,
his battered look just right
for those damaged vegetables.

Behind his table, he doesn't hawk so much
as grumble, husbandlike,
at the meager spread in front of him,
all day sitting over it
like a meal gone cold.

Beyond Us

Because I cannot imagine it
you sketch the news in cross-section:
the horizontal is the earth,
the hollow is the huge hole
left by the roots.
Above the ground you draw
the felled trunk like a sleeping giant,
the ball of roots its head,
its hairs pulled taut
by the earth in the cavity.
A drawing, words—

Can they explain how a tree
chopped and bulldozed an hour before,
a five-foot stump
that a farmer left lying in a wheat field,
can stand again
or explain the laws of nature
and of chance
by which an uprooted trunk
can snap back into place
and with its resurrection
bury his two children?

Public Portraits

1

His jacket worn at the elbows
waiting
in the cold for a bus

he rubs
two sticks together.
One of them breaks.

Leaning
on the signpost
two hands cupped

over nose and mouth
he blows out
his own fire.

2

On a gray day in the park
this gray man
folded over a newspaper

only hopes to grow
like the miracle of grass
taller in the rain.

Instead he straightens out
stiff
as a park bench.

On the Ganges
near the Burning Ghats

Midriver the boatman stops
to let the pilgrims bathe.
She stays on board with him
listening to the rain
on the small boat's canopy.

On the sand
a crowd is watching
two bundles tied to wood.
Wet wrapping clings to them,
disguising nothing:

a woman all in red,
a man in white.
Thin and rigid,
they're like matchsticks
burned once then thrown away.

Silent in the boat
he's waiting for the bathers.
He doesn't watch the banks
for fire or smoke
as she does.

Slipping

They say you're slipping.
While you sleep your hair changes color.

For more than sixty years
you argued with the mirror,

over the same washbasin
berated cold pipes to bring warm water.

Always in a hurry,
stirring soup, blowing clouds from a spoon,

until your knife comes down to the bare plate.
Chairs back away from the table

and right before your eyes, the house empties
the way an old dog loses teeth.

Today you stare
with the houseplant out the window.

Leaves are covering your lawn,
but you wear your hands in your pockets,

fingers stiff and pale
as the leftover stalks on the hydrangea.

When a plane soars by
you listen to the panes rattle.

Incandescence

In the morning she opens the door
for the newspaper.
Nothing else gets in,
except a rare piece of mail

and that box of groceries
on the front porch,
not even the boy who leaves them.
He never sees her.

On the back porch
the stacks of yellowed papers
and the green bottles covering the floor
mark the months like notches.

Behind the curtains
she needs incandescence in the afternoon
sipping on solitude,
reading the good parts to herself.

A Physical Examination

In the waiting room
an old magazine trembles.
Faces disappear
like breadcrumbs
left for the birds.

Outside the wind
must be peeling the sycamore,
one sleeve at a time.
I might as well start
with the buttons.

On this small hook
I leave all my coverings
and smiles.
Appearances no longer matter.
You take photographs in the dark.

Cold in a paper sheet
that won't fit
on this stiff bed I wait
like a lover
for the key in the door.

My tongue lies down
on the wet floor
in the cave,
a slippery rock
where the stick and light explore.

And this metal foot
hopping slowly
like a robin over my lawn
with a head bent
listens for the worm in my chest.

Maybe the young girl
bottling blood
already knows,
like a squirrel
when the peach softens on the limb.

Dressed again,
my socks drooping at my ankles,
I have just enough body
to hold up a head.
Small change rattles in my pocket.

Diagnosis

A lizard
runs across the ceiling
over my bed
leaving messages I can't decipher.

I wait
my ear to the ground
for symptoms.
Not even a bluejay coughs.

Only my name on test-tubes
sealed at the lips,
dark red icicles
lining my cave.

You're the unfaithful lover
coming late
full of words
and roses without roots.

You smile
a scarecrow to the wind
while the cat stalks my garden
and seedlings bow down behind my back.

Disease

One fly
trapped in the house
disturbs my sleep
like a bullet ricocheting off the window.

I feed balloons
to a hungry sky,
work all night like a seamstress
humming under my breath.

I plead
for a few gray hairs,
a new coat from the locust
but you won't listen.

You whisper
in the dark
like an overwatered plant.
A green rumor spreads.

By morning
I will be a mountain
and feed the sparrows
in the valley of my palm.

Under a Doctor's Care

I keep wishing you'd go away.
Maybe you're the gardener
who leaves the peony
leaning on its stem.

I want to be the girl
sunning herself,
wreathing a field of dandelions
on her lap and later on a bench

the old woman
watching the birds feed
on the mulberries' blood.
I wish you'd look the other way.

Recurring Symptoms

Disease comes at noon.
When I lean against the southern wall
I'm one with the shadow.

Some days I am afraid to move.
If the wind stirs
the nest sways high in the birch.

I rest on the ground
reading from my palms
the short-lived creases of the grass.

My nights grow dizzy
near the water.
I can almost hear the splashing.

Every morning I wipe the dust
from my eyes.
I wind my watch.

The Approach

A shovel scrapes snow from the walk.
When you come
you'll bring the cold air on your coat.

Confined to bed I listen
for my heart, the doorknob slowly twisting,
a blanket spreading its wings over me.

I count the cracks in the wall,
the years of dust
darkening the light fixture on the ceiling.

I get my words ready,
like a young girl, writing love poems
to no one.

I try my only psalm.
I'm at a wishbone, bare and brittle,
where there is no second chance.

Should I speak first? Or will disease,
like an impatient lover,
interrupt and change the subject?

Standing near me
backlit only by the moon
you are all silhouette, a faceless caller.

And I wait,
with all these tired roses,
for you to sweep the petals into a cupped hand.

Outpatient

A man in slippers
paces back and forth
holding a glass of water.

Now it's my turn
for the wheelchair.
Pedestrians avert their eyes.

I'm the crone
sagging on a park bench.
Pigeons squabble near my feet.

My hands grow cold
on my lap.
The half-moons huddle under cuticles.

When schoolboys hiss and run
I hear acorns
laughing at their shoes.

The Only Cure

A nurse takes my shoes.
One foot at a time, I test the bed.
It's an icy lake.
She leaves me floating on my back,
only my head above the surface.

Polished cutlery is spread on clean linen.
Table or bed?
And these green gowns and masks? I'm not fooled—
their gloves are thin, transparent as skin.
This is no party.

Whispering approaches.
Should I resist
or let them bind me to this tree?
Ten eyes form a circle, but I don't flinch.
I must be spellbound.

Whiteness hovers overhead.
It could be the winter sky
or maybe it's the surgeon's light.
It doesn't matter which—I close my eyes.
Darkness is the only cure.

Convalescence

On a white beach
littered with shells and seaweed
flung ashore by a watery hand
I rest

a damaged thing
beneath this blue bruise of the sky
sand in my bed
waves spreading sheets over me

no more than driftwood
I'm a tree
that lost its footing
an invalid the water washes.

A Pillow of Stone

In those days
a man could rest his head
on a pillow of stone.
He could see the ladder in a dream.
When the angels came
a man would entertain them,
wash their feet and feed them bread
in the shade of a tree.

Once in a dream
sheaves bowed down to a boy,
so did the stars.
A king had visions and interpreters.
No secrets troubled them.
Then a man could hear the voice
in the garden, in the mountains,
or even in a burning bush.

Such tales live on
in our brick house.
When you cry
that a rock falls in your sleep
we console you.
Still a dream can grow
dark as a bruise
and hurt for days.

Tooth and Nail

"Every tooth in a man's head is more valuable than a diamond."
—Miguel de Cervantes

Last night my necklace broke.
Bending in a dream, I heard silk tear at the seams.
I filled my palm with pearls, all knobby and yellow.

Now as I bite this thread in two,
the spool jumps off my lap.
One palm stays in the dream, one on my skirt.

Slowly turned, its blue veins rise.
The skin sits loosely on its back, like this old sweater.
I grow a size too small for myself.

Nothing fits.
Not even this shelf in the pantry.
Lately I have to stand on my toes to reach it.

I save my voice, but this single-minded tongue
keeps circling over my losses.
I count the teeth-marks in my apple and make do.

Maybe tonight you will come like a lost word
or a coin under my pillow.
I watch my fingernails return.

Living Room

Often crossing our living room
I picture that woman
amidst her moss-green upholstery,
her worn gray rug,

the last occupant, hunched, white-haired,
who, while you slowed the shutter speed,
walked through as I do now.
In one door, out the other.

For all our years,
painting, dusting, polishing,
for all our carpets, curtains,
tables, chairs, and knickknacks,

I'm like the white blur
across the photograph in our album,
already half-ghost
in this room borrowed from time.

Background

"The background of his discontent is embedded in the legend
of the Four Passing Sights."

—Huston Smith

Remember her visits—
her teeth and the morning bubbles
in that glass of water near her bed

and at the breakfast table
the lemon in a cup of steaming water, the Old World
in that sugar cube melting on her tongue,

her lips whispering behind the newspaper,
her cheeks caving in
when we caught her at it.

Remember those large black bedroom-slippers
shuffling on linoleum, clearing our dishes
from the table to the sink—

those thick peasant legs,
dark veins bulging at the back,
red blotches where the ankles rubbed

and when she sat
ungirdled in that flowered house-dress
remember how her lap spread

and above that neckline
how skin hung loosely at her throat—
remember thinking we were different?

Premonition

In the next house
someone is moving away.
All day I can hear the door rehearsing.

Other feet will drag the mud
through this house;
other hands will sweep it.

They will change the sheets
like the weeks,
hang new curtains in the windows

and on cold afternoons
will watch the wet names of children
running down the glass.

On the same threshold
someone else will turn her face
to shake out the rug of memory,

will dust under a different table
and put the chairs back
like established facts.

Nothing here belongs to us:
the lace, the linens in the drawers,
they have begun their yellow return.

I know without looking.
Behind the ice of this mirror
a whole world melts.

At the dinner table
when you pass the plate
I smell a stranger's house.

Playing from Memory

Mother had never played for us—
not once. I was practicing
when she sat next to me on the bench.
Without a word
she began that burst of music,
her vein-backed hands
making the keys ripple, waking
her childhood in our living room.

She seldom played after that
even if we coaxed
and then only that one piece. Always
the beginning would come back to her
and always at the same arpeggio that stumbling,
starting again, stumbling—those few notes
like the name of the piece
always escaping her. She would stand

to lower the fall-board, hinge by hinge.
Everytime it happened—
not just the music breaking in half
or that chord like framed glass
shattering in place
or even the wood clanking against wood
but the silence afterward—
the keyboard closed on all our pasts.

Survivors

While we were sipping,
slowly emptying our glasses,
snow buried these streets.
We could be the lone survivors,
the last pulse of a beast
that this midnight wind circles
like a hawk.

All the way home I keep hearing hymns
in the hum our trudging makes,
on our white breath
the prayers, the chanting
of our ancestors—their hopes fed
on the same hard crusts
we scattered to the birds.

On our lawn a tall birch bows
nearly to the ground.
It blocks our way.
We brush off the snow, limb by limb,
till the whole tree
whips the night in front of us
grazing our coats, missing our faces.

In the Rock-Carved Church at Göreme

Right below this ridge, the white cones loom
like leviathans punished into stone.
Their dark windows gape at us.

Inside, the windows light the faded murals.
Where faces were,
bare rock stares from the chips.

We have to crawl one at a time
to find the shaft,
head down, as the monks did centuries ago,

then climb
straight up for twelve or fourteen feet.
First the guide goes.

Right under him, I stand,
torso in the tunnel, feet still on the ground
and he, astride the very air, is scaling,

cheering down like Orpheus
until a swerve absorbs him, voice and all.
It's dark.

Saint Hieron hid from Romans in the labyrinth.
If the Turkish boy is right,
he used the same treads beneath my fingers,

powdery and narrow.
I breathe the ancient dust.
I hear the litany of stones and stay behind.

Cleaning Indian Dahl

If you watch me
picking stones out of these red lentils
pushing the tiny peas, grain by grain
across a white platter
you'll find it tedious

unless you know
that it takes more for someone else
to put them in, than for me to take them out,
that each rock was chosen carefully
by size, by color

and that the way a butcher
might rest his thumb on a scale
some man or woman, maybe even a child
boosted a poor yield
with this grit in my palm.

To the Uninvited

Her party, dear,
is the same party that we read about:
twelve golden plates in the palace,
thirteen fairies in the kingdom.
There's never enough to go around.
Someone makes a list,
someone else is uninvited.
A wish turns to a curse, a fairy
to a witch—you know the rest:
the pricking rage,
the whole court in its spell,
a century behind a thorn hedge
to sleep it off,
to let a kiss through. Remember, too,
taking Sleeping Beauty's side,
slighting the witch so willingly?
Such an easeful story then—
nothing cautionary, nothing real,
none of us in it.

By Accident

Because I brought him here
I hold his hand
while the surgeon cleans his leg,
a boy I hardly know, a child
my daughter's age. Years ago
a black nurse held
my white hand in a hospital and I
squeezed then just as he does now
a stranger never thanked
never forgotten.

I know how it happens,
how pain softens us as easily
as habit hardens, how
we meet now and if we meet again
we both avert our eyes,
the boy and I,
as from the gash itself,
the white seams gaping on the raw red,
we turn away. Often I think we can,
given half a chance, love anyone.

On the Courtois River

At one bend the river narrowed
till the bluffs surrounded us.
We held our paddles in the boat
listening to the dark,
watching as a child does from bed.

Now both banks are low.
We watch the rocks on the riverbed
till the ripples over them
distract us
the way waves do in an old window.

We don't mind
the water covering our path
or the rapids drowning out our voices.
Nothing stands still.
Even the land slips by like a minnow.

Thin trees, already leafless,
are fingering the clear October sky.
They're getting nothing.
On the ridge against that pale backdrop
two cows are reduced to silhouette.

Out here we don't mind oblivion
or where the water widens into silence.
Nothing interrupts.
Even the sky yawns down
on the solitary snag that's beckoning.

Partial Vision

At noon I eat my lunch in silence
on the back porch steps.
Maybe birds will come for the crusts.

The sun beats down on the grass.
Bright green, it glares
from a night of rain that I slept through.

The daffodils wither and wrinkle.
Under a wide-brimmed hat, I hide
blinded to the branches and the sky.

But I can see a whole flock of shadows
sweeping back and forth
in a sudden blessing over the lawn.

Refuge

This sycamore leaks.
It's a pauper's house
where the rain loosens old paint
from the walls.

Huddled near the trunk
I can hear squirrels in the attic
back and forth
over the empty rafters.

My feet sink
into a perfect fit of leaves.
I wear the damp shoes
discarded by winter.

Rain closes my eyes.
I see a green parasol
instead of that white umbrella
torn and inverted by the wind.

Autumnal Equinox

While I dry the dinner dishes
she crayons on my stationery,
a get-well card. She asks without looking up
how the leaves know when to fall
but doesn't listen.

She seals the envelope on the subject,
rubs it with her small palm for emphasis
and pushes it aside.
She doesn't want to know about the equinox
or her grandmother

just as I don't want to hear
these plates clattering or know
in this dusk between my child's innocence
and my mother's illness—what my hand
knows first on the cold ribs of this radiator.

The way today is equal to tonight
my life now must be equal
to its dark time; in this kitchen,
at this sink, love must be the axis
that our years spin around.

The Names of the Birds

Our children clamor on the lawn
shrieking, banging forks on pots
to scare the birds out of the peaches.

At bedtime they go inside
leaving their shoes under the tree,
their half-filled baskets on the steps.

Facing east, we watch a pair of honey locusts,
the last light on their top branches,
while night rises from the ground like dark water.

It's true—so much escapes us.
Until you mentioned it
I hadn't noticed that the birds were gone.

Cardinals, bluejays, robins, sparrows,
I name them in the dark
like articles of faith,

knowing each bird
is one of those wishes spent so carelessly
in my own fairytale.

It's also true
that tomorrow even without us
the sky will invent its birds again.

Looking Both Ways

for Don and Connie

Old leaves, the perfume of moldering,
dirt beneath my nails.
I want to empty all my pockets.

This is my house to sweep.
Even the crumbs in the corner
belong to me.

In this closet
for each velvet dress on a hanger
at least one night danced.

All these glasses poured wine.
These dusty dishes
sat on lace and linen tables.

All night back and forth
over a street light's glare
the curtain swings.

Somewhere a door must be fanning the air,
someone practicing an exit,
a girl looking both ways.